This Little Tiger book
belongs to:

_____

_____

_____

_____

D0193319

*For those who shine bright in the
darkest of times ~ O H*

*For Gideon Algernon Mantell (famous historical
palaeontologist) and also his namesake Gideon Algernon
Mantell (my pet dog Algy — who one day may start
digging up old bones himself) ~ S J*

LITTLE TIGER PRESS LTD,
an imprint of the Little Tiger Group
1 Coda Studios, 189 Munster Road,
London SW6 6AW
www.littletiger.co.uk

First published in Great Britain 2019
This edition published 2020

Text by Owen Hart
Text copyright © Little Tiger Press Ltd 2019
Illustrations copyright © Sean Julian 2019
Sean Julian has asserted his right to be identified as the illustrator
of this work under the Copyright, Designs and Patents Act, 1988
A CIP catalogue record for this book is available
from the British Library

Owen Hart

Sean Julian

I LOVE YOU BRIGHTER THAN THE STARS

LITTLE TIGER
LONDON

When sunlight fades and shadows fall,
come walk awhile with me.
We'll watch the sky as stars appear
and count each one we see.

And as we saunter, side by side,
the gentle moon above,
I'll whisper softly just how much
you fill my heart with love.

Look, over there: tonight's first star!
Its twinkle lights our way.
And I will do the same, my love –
I'll be your guide each day.

Will there be more? Oh yes, I'm sure.
Why don't we climb this hill?
I'll be beside you, every step,
just like I always will.

And there it is: a second star!
It shimmers bright and true –
A light that shines forevermore,
just like my love for you.

The third star, near the mountain's peak,
is brighter than the rest.
However far away you roam
you always will be blessed . . .

. . . For even if we're parted
we'll both wish upon that star,
And sure enough my love
will find a path to where you are.

At last, we reach the mountain top
and gasp with pure delight,
For stretching out before us
is an awe-inspiring sight . . .

The heavens glow with light
as every star comes out to play.
And all at once we feel more joy
than words could ever say.

Let's take a dip and chase the stars
reflected in the stream.
We leap and splash and giggle
as the dancing waters gleam.

Too many stars to count, you say
and give a little yawn.
It's time for bed, so home we go
to rest until the dawn.

Let's snuggle down and listen
to the wind's soft lullaby.
I'll kiss your cheek and say goodnight
beneath our starry sky.

Remember this, my precious one:
you shine so very bright.

I love you more than all the stars
that sparkle through the night.

More books you'll love
from Little Tiger . . .